HOSEA PLAYS ON

BY
KATHLEEN M. BLASI

ILLUSTRATED BY
SHANE W. EVANS

STERLING CHILDREN'S BOOKS
New York

Hosea tucked his shiny brass saxophone in its
velvet-lined case and glanced at the wakening sky.
On a day like this, he thought, *I could play forever*.
He smiled. Maybe—just maybe—he would
earn enough today.

He stepped outside.
Nate, his neighbor, looked up from
raking leaves with his dad.

"MORNIN'!"

they called. Nate lifted the
rake handle to his lips and
pretended to play.

KA-
PLINK-
PLINK-
PLINK-
PLINK.

The city scrolled past,
each stop bringing him closer
to the public market.

Hosea waited for
the Number 25,
then dropped in
his coins.

(change)

SCREEECH-WHOOSH. SQUEEEEEAK. SHHHHHH.

Hosea clomped down the steps and shuffled through brittle, dancing leaves. He stepped through the market's archway and shooed cooing pigeons that were scrounging for breakfast.

Hosea made his way to his favorite playing spot, near a coffee shop. Beneath gathering clouds, folks streamed into the market. Hosea settled in, opened his case, and pulled out his saxophone. He took a deep breath, then released a tune, long and low.

Fingers fluttered. Keys clicked. Smoky notes lifted through the air, threading along to waiting ears.

People slowed, then stopped, to listen to the melody

STRETCH . . . . . . CLIMB . . . .

SOAR . . .
.
AND
FALL.

Some folks sat on the ground. Some dropped money in Hosea's case.
His eyes crinkled with joy, and he kept on. Between songs,
a woman asked him how long he'd been playing.

"This old thing?" Hosea asked. "Not as long as my *first* love."
The woman raised her eyebrows.

As the sun ducked behind darkening clouds, a little girl stepped forward. She began to sway. The crowd hushed. She dipped and twirled, her toes a sweeping whisper.

When the song was over, the girl curtsied, then poised for their next duet. But a peppering rain scattered the crowd to a nearby pavilion.

HOSEA PLAYED ON.

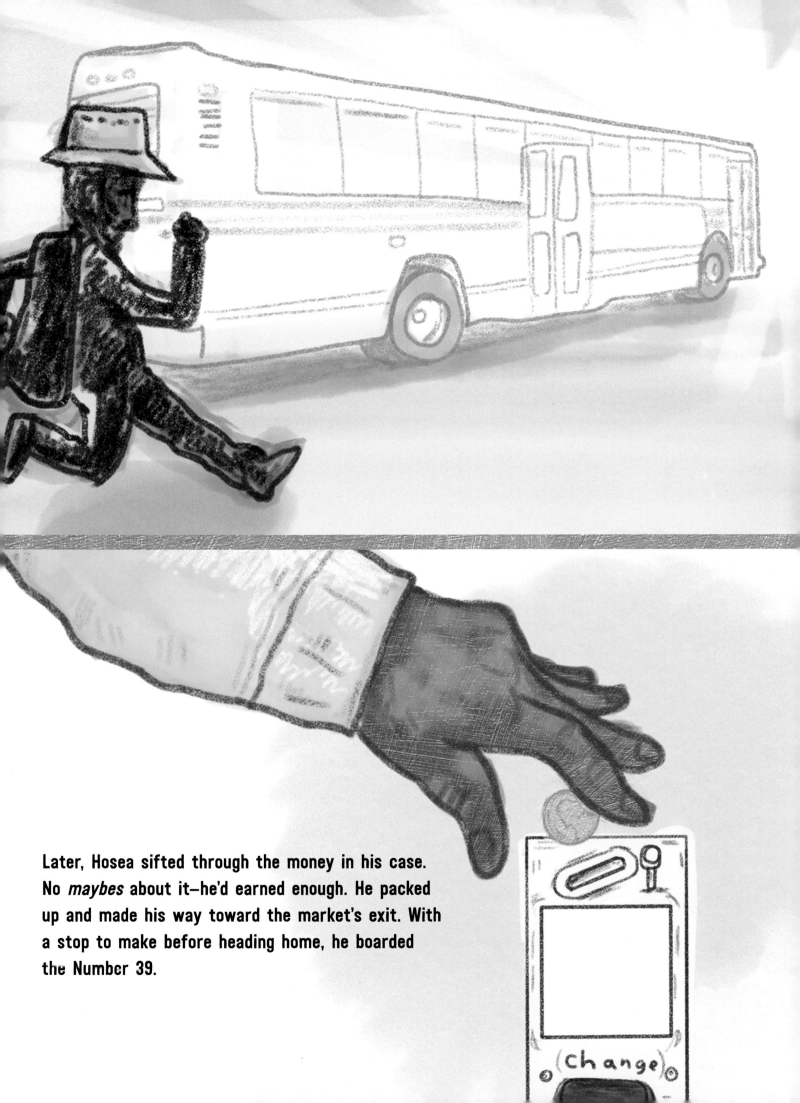

Later, Hosea sifted through the money in his case. No *maybes* about it—he'd earned enough. He packed up and made his way toward the market's exit. With a stop to make before heading home, he boarded the Number 39.

The music shop's door squeaked his arrival.
"Good afternoon, Hosea!" Ms. May waved him in.
"What'll it be today?"

"HOW ABOUT A NICE TRUMPET-TO-GO?"

"How many trumpet players does that band of yours need?" Ms. May teased.

"ALWAYS ROOM FOR ONE MORE,"

answered Hosea. He chose one he thought was just right.

Near home, Hosea stepped onto the sidewalk.
He listened to the music of the day—the scritch-
scratch of leaves, the whistle of wind, the groan
of a nearby bridge as a truck passed over it.
     With one hand hidden behind his back,
Hosea watched Nate march toward him.

"How'd it go, Mr. Hosea?"
"Like this. Nate, put that phony horn away."
Hosea pulled the trumpet case from behind his back.

"BECAUSE NOW YOU HAVE A REAL ONE TO PLAY!"

Nate's face lit up. "For me? Thank you!"
He clutched the case to his chest.
"Will you teach me, too?"

"Depends," answered Hosea.
"You ready to learn?"

They settled on the stoop. Hosea lifted the shiny brass trumpet from its velvet-lined case and handed it to Nate. The boy drew in a breath, then released a tangled tune.

Together, the two played on.

For my parents, Frank and Gloria McAlpin, whose
circle of kindness always has room for one more. —K.M.B.

I thank God for the vision and hands to guide me.
This book is dedicated to the memory of Pat Dougherty and his family,
to all who graced the School of the Arts and Monroe High School,
and to the city of Rochester, NY, that we all called home,
the city that made "Hosea Play" and all of us play along. —S.W.E.

ACKNOWLEDGMENTS

Thank you to the Rochester, New York community,
whose love of Hosea inspired me in writing this story.

STERLING CHILDREN'S BOOKS
New York

An Imprint of Sterling Publishing Co., Inc.
1166 Avenue of the Americas
New York, NY 10036

Text © 2019 Kathleen M. Blasi
Illustrations © 2019 Shane W. Evans

ISBN 978-1-4549-2683-2

Distributed in Canada by Sterling Publishing Co., Inc.
C/o Canadian Manda Group, 664 Annette Street
Toronto, Ontario M6S 2C8, Canada
Distributed in the United Kingdom by GMC Distribution Services
Castle Place, 166 High Street, Lewes, East Sussex BN7 1XU, England
Distributed in Australia by NewSouth Books
University of New South Wales, Sydney, NSW 2052, Australia

For information about custom editions, special sales, and
premium and corporate purchases, please contact Sterling Special Sales
at 800-805-5489 or specialsales@sterlingpublishing.com.

Manufactured in China

Lot #:
2   4   6   8   10   9   7   5   3   1
10/19

sterlingpublishing.com